Selma's Purple Hair

Rawan Dashti

Illustrated By Farah Khaleel

Illustrated by Farah Khaleel.

Balboa Press books may be ordered through booksellers or by contacting:

Balboa Press
A Division of Hay House
1663 Liberty Drive
Bloomington, IN 47403
www.balboapress.com
1 (877) 407-4847

ISBN: 978-1-5043-5705-0 (sc)
ISBN: 978-1-5043-5707-4 (e)

Library of Congress Control Number: 2016906977

Print information available on the last page.

Balboa Press rev. date: 05/27/2016

Selma's Purple Hair

Rawan Dashti
Illustrated By Farah Khaleel

In a land not far from here,
Lived a girl called Selma.
She had very long and curly hair,
The color of pearly purple.

Selma was ready to go to school,
For the very first time.
She felt excited and happy,
And oh! So sublime.

When Selma arrived to class that day,
She was completely shocked!
All the girls had short pink hair,
As straight as candy stalks.

Selma felt so very different,
From all the other girls.
This feeling was not pleasant at all,
She suddenly hated her curls.

She hated the color purple,
And wanted desperately to change.
She wanted to be the same as them,
Not different, not strange.

Back home she cut off her long long strands,
With a big pair of scissors.
She dipped them in a pail of pink paint,
And pressed them to get straightened.

Pink

As soon as Selma thought she was done,
Something outrageous happened.
Her hair began turning purple again,
And grew longer than before and curlier.

That night before she went to bed,
Selma gazed into the sky.
She closed her eyes and made a wish,
Then saw a butterfly.

The butterfly fluttered it's pretty wings,
And entered Selma's room.
"I have granted you your wish," it said,
Then up and away it flew.

Selma ran to the mirror on her wall,
And stared in disbelief.
Most certainly her hair had changed,
It was short, straight, and pink!

The next day at school all the girls,
Wanted to be her friend.
She looked exactly like everybody else,
And blended in so well.

One day not very long from that,
A production came to town.
They were scouting dancers for the next big play,
And Selma put her name down.

At the audition for the play,
She put a lot of effort into the act.
She danced and sang the leading part
And waited for the judges to react.

All of them gave her a big thumbs up,
Except for the main producer.
"Your skills are promising," she said,
"But you have nothing unique to offer."

"If only you looked a little bit different,
Than all the other girls.
That would make me extremely happy.
Otherwise, you do have great skills."

Selma was extremely heart broken,
So that night before she slept,
She wished to see the butterfly again,
And maybe ask for help.

The butterfly flew in through her window,
Just like the first time around.
“How can I help you dear Selma?” she asked,
As her wings fluttered up and down.

“I need my old image back!” cried Selma,
My curly purple hair.
I need to be unique and different,
So I’ll be cast in this year’s play.”

“Im sorry,” said the butterfly,
“That wish is just not possible.
This image is what you wished to be,
So accept it, I know you’re capable.”

Selma felt tears run down her cheeks,
As the butterfly flew away.
"I will do anything," she thought to herself,
"Anything to be cast in that play."

That night she did not sleep a wink,
Until morning rays peeked through the window.
She had worked tirelessly on a homemade wig,
And was planning to put on a show.

She showed up for the audition again,
But with curly, purple hair instead.
She performed the leading part and twirled,
But the wig flew right off her head!

"It looks wonderful," the producer said,
Pointing to the wig.
"If only it was real and stuck,
It would have been a big hit."

"Why must you focus," Selma cried,
"So much on how I look?
Why can't you search deeper?
You will be surprised with what you find:

I possess a heart as clear as glass,
And kindness is my wealth.
I dance and sing so beautifully,
But it's only on looks that you dwell."

And exactly then the producer herself,
Transformed into the butterfly,
"My dear Selma," she said with a smile,
"You fill my heart with pride.

You have learnt life's most important lesson:
How you look is not the issue.
Everyone possesses a different beauty,
That reflects their innermost ESSENCE.

That was the last of the butterfly,
Selma would ever see.
She never made another wish,
And was happy just as SHE.

You do the same my dear dear friend,
Be happy with who YOU are.
Enjoy the outside and the inside,
And find joy, peace and love.

CPSIA information can be obtained
at www.ICGtesting.com
Printed in the USA
LVHW07s2351010318
568396LV00007B/42/P

9 781504 357050